Alpacas with Maracas

MATT COSGROVE

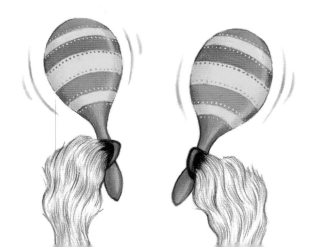

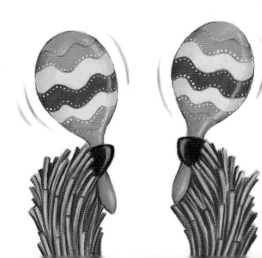

First published in 2018 by Koala Books
An imprint of Scholastic Australia Pty Limited

First published in the UK in 2020 by Scholastic Children's Books
Euston House, 24 Eversholt Street
London, NW1 1DB
A division of Scholastic Ltd
www.scholastic.co.uk

London ~ New York ~ Toronto ~ Sydney ~ Auckland
Mexico City ~ New Delhi ~ Hong Kong

Text and illustrations copyright © Matt Cosgrove 2018

Typeset in Mr Dodo featuring Festivo LC.

This guy is called **Macca.**

He's an alpaca!

He likes **eating**...

PICKLES

And loves getting . . .

tickles!

That guy is called **Al.**
He's Macca's best pal.

He's an alpaca too.
(With a **shaggy** hair do.)

Al has a **BIG** heart...

‘Oh! Oh! Oh! Oh!’

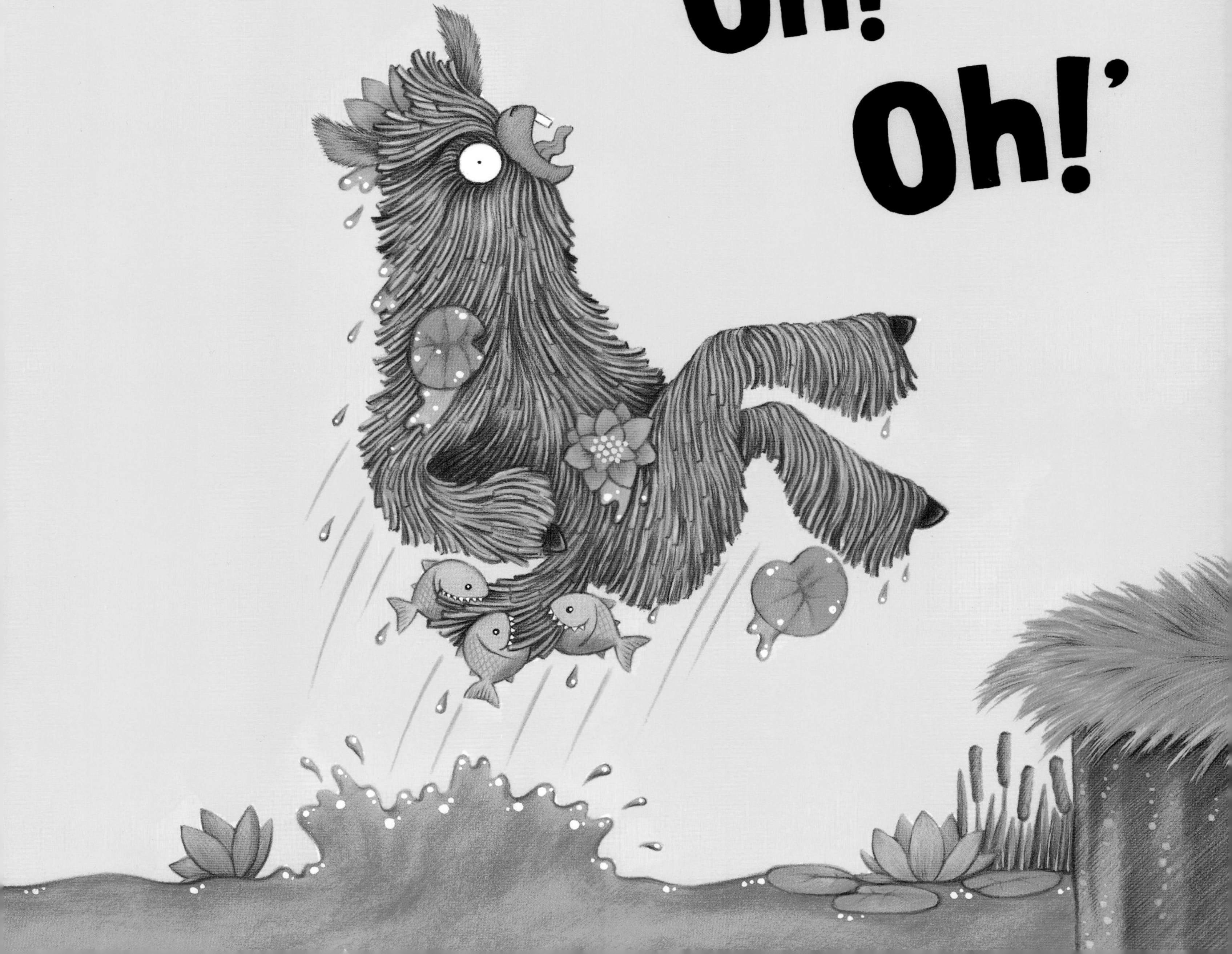

These **buddies** are tight.

From morning to night.

Always looking for ways,
to **brighten** their days.

'A talent show.
Let's give it a go!'

Al said with a grin,
'I **BET** we could **WIN!**'

Macca beamed back,
'All we need is an **act!**'

So, most earnest and gallant,
They searched for their talent.

They tried **strumming**,

And **drumming**,

And **crashing**,

But the cuddly duo, were utterly so-so.

Their magic was **tragic.**

Their choir was **dire.**

Their tumbling was **bumbling.**

Their falling

APPALLING!

'It's hopeless!' Al hissed,
And then he shook his fist.

Macca stared at his pal,
'You're a genius Al!

We can't sing or play brother,
But we can shake like no other.

We don't need a big fracas!
**We
just
*need...'***

On talent show day,
They began to sashay.

They **shimmied**, they **grooved**. They **wiggled**, they **moved**.

Chika chika cha cha cha!

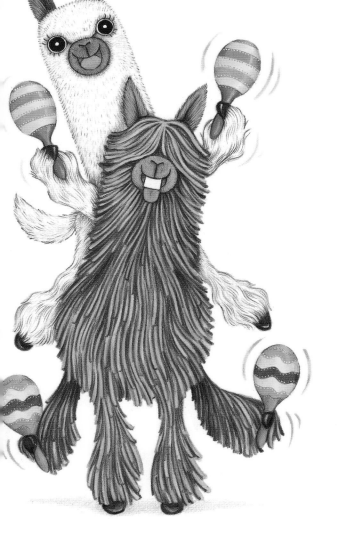

Ticka ticka ta ta ta!

Well the crowd all went **crackers,**

For the **alpacas with maracas**

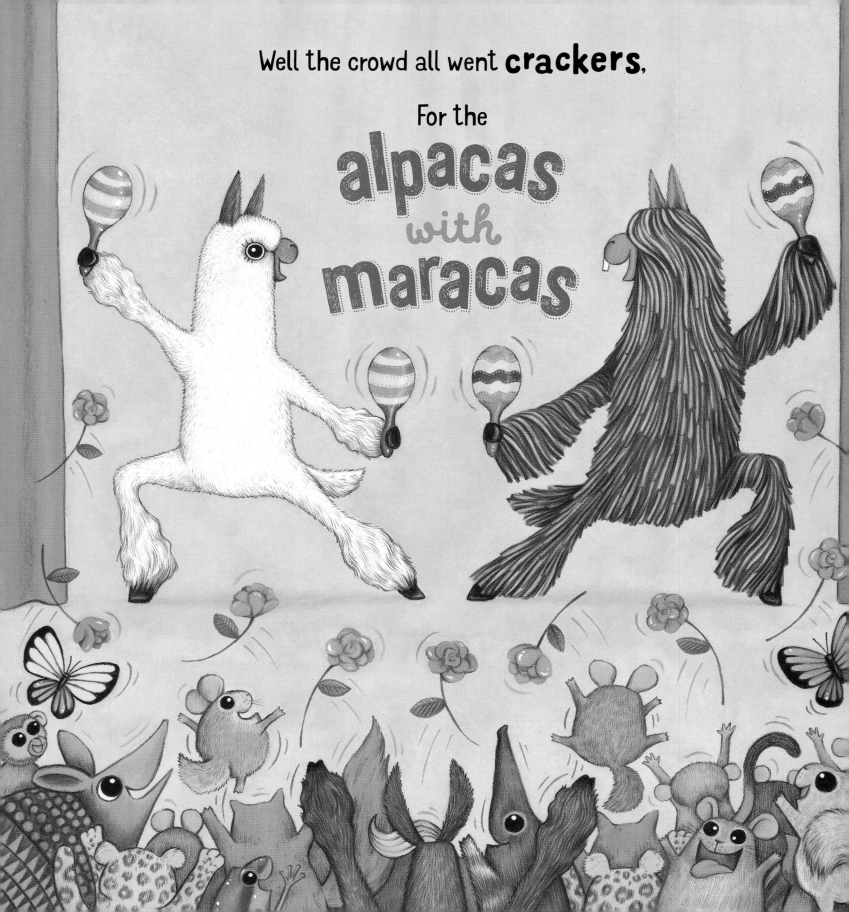

The pair had a **blast!**
Even though they came **LAST.**

Then they shook to the max,

with the **yaks playing sax!**